DINOSAUR ROAR!

For John Smith

DINOSAUR ROAR!
A PICTURE CORGI BOOK 978 0 552 56936 1
First published in Great Britain in 1994 by Ragged Bears Publishing Ltd.
This edition published in Great Britain in 2014 by Picture Corgi,
an imprint of Random House Children's Publishers UK
A Random House Group Company

1 3 5 7 9 10 8 6 4 2

Text copyright © Henrietta Stickland, 1994
Illustrations copyright © Paul Stickland, 1994

RANDOM HOUSE CHILDREN'S PUBLISHERS UK
61–63 Uxbridge Road, London W5 5SA

www.**randomhousechildrens**.co.uk
www.**randomhouse**.co.uk
www.dinosaurroar.com

Addresses for companies within The Random House Group Limited can be found at:
www.randomhouse.co.uk/offices.htm
THE RANDOM HOUSE GROUP Limited Reg. No. 954009
A CIP catalogue record for this book is available from the British Library.

Printed in China

The Random House Group Limited supports the Forest Stewardship Council® (FSC®), the leading
international forest-certification organisation. Our books carrying the FSC label are printed on FSC®-certified paper.
FSC is the only forest-certification scheme supported by the leading environmental organisations, including Greenpeace.
Our paper procurement policy can be found at www.randomhouse.co.uk/environment

MIX
Paper from
responsible sources
FSC
www.fsc.org
FSC® C104723

DINOSAUR ROAR!

PAUL STICKLAND   HENRIETTA STICKLAND

PUBLISHED IN ASSOCIATION WITH
THE NATURAL HISTORY MUSEUM

PICTURE CORGI

Dinosaur roar,

dinosaur squeak,

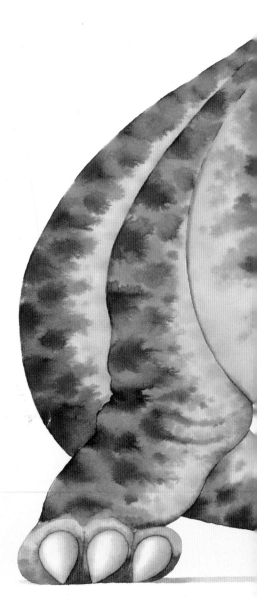

dinosaur fierce,

dinosaur meek,

dinosaur fast,

dinosaur slow,

dinosaur above

and dinosaur below.

Dinosaur weak,

dinosaur strong,

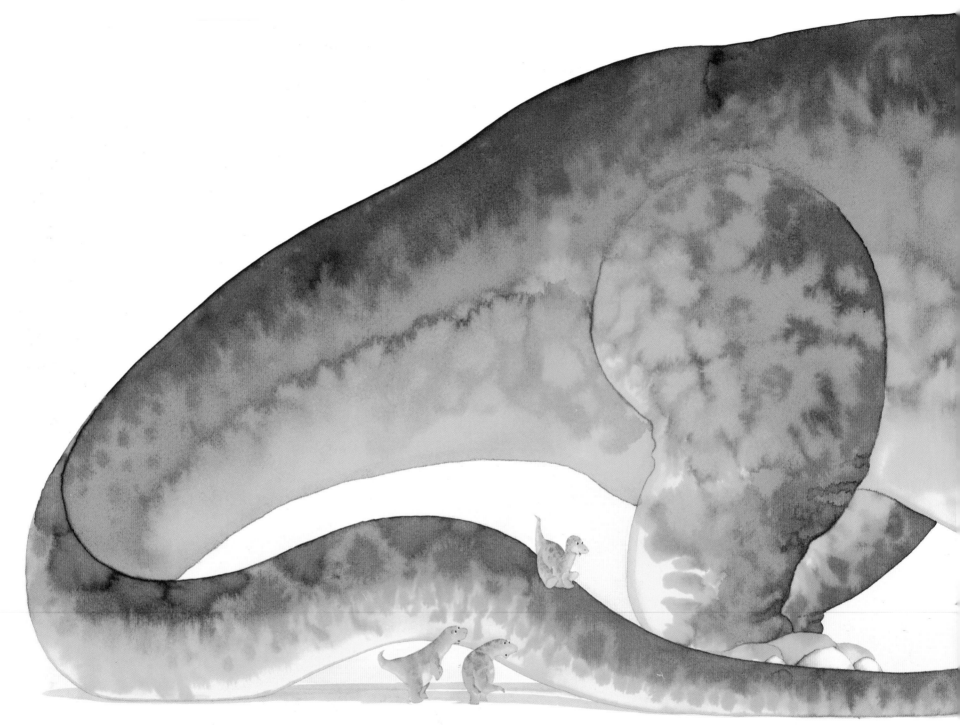

dinosaur short

or very, very long.

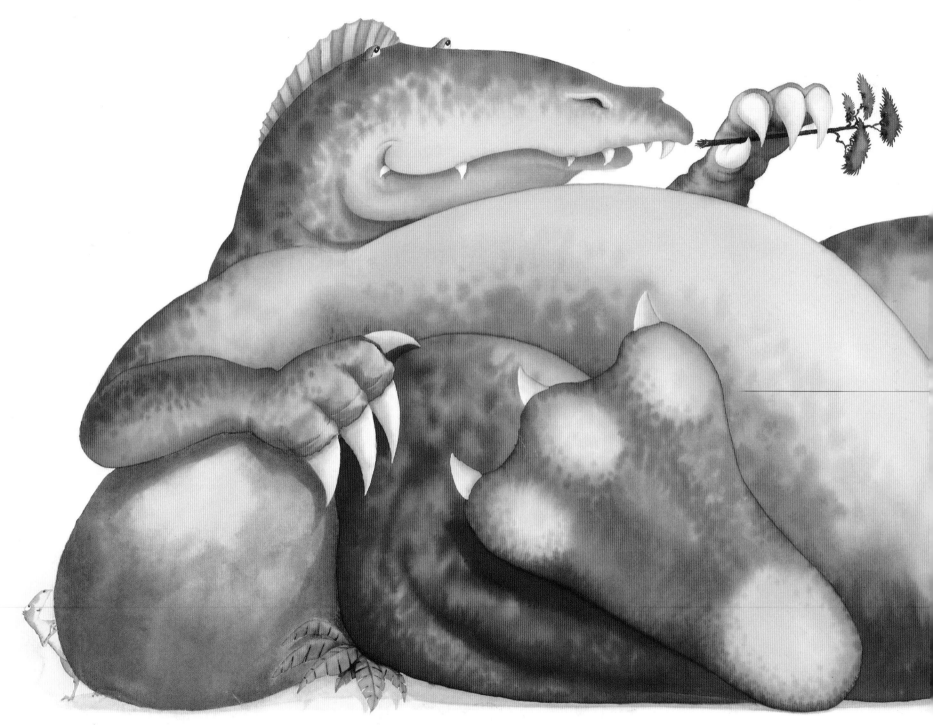

Dinosaur fat,

dinosaur tiny,

dinosaur clean

and dinosaur slimy.

Dinosaur sweet,

dinosaur grumpy,

dinosaur spiky

and dinosaur lumpy.

All sorts of dinosaurs

eating up their lunch,

gobble, gobble, nibble, nibble,

munch, munch, scrunch!

Discover a whole world
of dinosaurs at
www.dinosaurroar.com